Amanda
in
england

THE MISSING NOVEL

darlene foster

To marin
Happy reading!
Darlene
Foster
☺

central
avenue
publishing

2012

Amanda in England: The Missing Novel

ISBN 978-1-926760-77-3

Published in Canada with international distribution.

Cover Design: Michelle Halket

Photography: Copyright & Courtesy of iStockphoto: brodiefoto

Original cover of A WORLD OF GIRLS, by L.T. Meade, illustrated by M. E. Edwards 3rd edition published by Cassell & Company 1887

Map of England: himmera.com

To

Aleasha, Amanda, Taylor and Jesse

My amazing grandchildren

England

- ⊙ National Capital
- International Boundary
- Provincial Boundary
- Devon Province Name

100 km

0 — 100 Miles

North Sea

SCOTLAND

NORTHERN IRELAND

ISLE OF MAN

Irish Sea

IRELAND

Northumberland

Tyne and Wear

Durham

Cleveland

Cumbria

North Yorkshire

Humberside

Lancashire

West Yorkshire

Greater Manchester

South Yorkshire

Merseyside

Cheshire

Derbyshire

Nottinghamshire

Lincolnshire

ENGLAND

Staffordshire

Leicestershire

Norfolk

Shropshire

West Midlands

WALES

Warwickshire

Northamptonshire

Cambridgeshire

Suffolk

Hereford and Worcester

Bedfordshire

Essex

Gloucestershire

Oxfordshire

Buckinghamshire

Hertfordshire

London

Avon

Berkshire

Greater London

Wiltshire

Surrey

Kent

Somerset

Hampshire

W. Sussex

E. Sussex

Devon

Dorset

Strait of Dover

Cornwall

Isle of Wight

English Channel

chapter 1

A manda peered out the window, through the mist, down onto smoking chimneys and blackened roofs. Her excitement grew as the airplane descended.

'Here I am, at last, in the land of the Potters – Beatrix and Harry,' Amanda thought as the plane lurched to a halt at Heathrow Airport, London.

She followed the other passengers to the luggage retrieval. Although she had only flown outside of Canada twice before, she felt quite comfortable with the process. She took her bag off the luggage carousel and proceeded to the customs gate.

"Hey you!" shouted someone behind her. Amanda turned to see a teenage girl with a bright pink Mohawk, tons of make up, earrings everywhere and a very short skirt. "You sure that's your bag?"

"Yes, I am." Amanda looked at the luggage tag. "See – here, this is my name."

"Um, so you're Amanda Ross – from Canada

I see." The girl examined the luggage tag. "Sorry t'bother you. Ta Ta. Stay out of trouble." She winked at Amanda with a dark lined eyelid, caked with mascara. She joined a teenage boy with tattooed arms wearing an England T-shirt and ripped jeans.

When Amanda emerged from customs, she found Leah and her dad waiting for her with balloons and flowers and a big sign that said, "Welcome to England, Amanda!"

"Wowza! Look at you," said Leah as she gave her a big hug. "I think you've grown."

"I don't know about that - but you sure have," said Amanda as she looked up at her tall, thin friend.

"Let's get you out of here," said Mr. Anderson as he took Amanda's bag from her. "I'm sure you're tired after the long flight and most likely hungry."

"It wasn't nearly as long a flight, as to the United Arab Emirates or even to Spain," replied Amanda.

She shivered when they got outside. With a slight drizzle, the air felt damp. Mr. Anderson led them to a shiny, silver-grey BMW. He put Amanda's bag in the trunk, went around to the passenger side and said, "You girls can sit in the back together. It's unlocked." He got in and sat in the passenger seat.

'That's weird,' thought Amanda. 'Who is going to drive? Do they have a chauffeur?'

It was when Mr. Anderson started the car; she

noticed the steering wheel on the right side. "Now, that is strange," she murmured.

They eventually found their way out of the busy airport parking lot. As Leah's dad turned to exit, he pulled into the wrong lane.

"Oh no!" Amanda squeezed her eyes shut for the inevitable head on collision.

"What's wrong, Amanda?" Leah asked with a concerned look.

"I thought we were going to have an accident." Amanda opened her eyes and looked out the window at the many cars driving toward them – on the opposite side of the road.

Leah's dad chuckled, "We drive on the left side of the road over here. I guess that must seem odd to you. You should be careful when crossing the street as you must look right, left and then right again."

Amanda breathed a sigh of relief. "That's weird, but good to know. I'll be careful. Even though you speak the same language here, there will be some things new and different, I guess."

Leah gave her arm a squeeze. "I'm so glad you're here. We'll have bags of fun. I can't wait to take you shopping at Harrods downtown. Mom said we can go on the London Eye too."

Amanda wanted to ask about the London Eye, but she was too tired and too excited as they drove through London towards the suburb of Guildford, where the Andersons lived. All the books she read about England flipped through her mind. Like her visits to the United Arab Emirates and Spain, she felt like she was living inside a novel. This was going to be the best spring break ever!

chapter 2

"Will we be going on the London Eye to-day?" asked Amanda after a good sleep.

"We will have to wait until you get back from the Isle of Wight," replied Mrs. Anderson. "Leah's dad needs to check on the boat and take it out for a trial run before the sailing races in two weeks."

"A boat? A sailboat? I've always wanted a ride on a sailboat." Amanda's eyes lit up.

"My husband will be happy to take you out for a ride if you wish. Leah isn't usually very keen." Mrs. Anderson put some cheese, bread and ham slices in a wicker basket.

"I don't know if I want a landlubber on board my boat," said Mr. Anderson, as he poured himself a coffee. "You can come along if you promise not to get in the way or fall overboard."

"I'll stay out of the way, I promise." Amanda wasn't sure if he was serious or not.

Amanda, Leah and Mr. Anderson drove to a large

city called Southampton and boarded a ferry which took them to the Isle of Wight. The murky, grey-blue water looked very different from the waters of the Persian Gulf or the Mediterranean Sea. Amanda spotted snowy white cliffs in the distance. "Is that where we're going?"

"Yep, that's the Isle of Wight," replied Leah.

'Makes sense,' thought Amanda, even though 'white' was spelled different.

Some teenagers walked past them. "Hi ya, Amanda from Canada," said a girl.

"Oh – hi," said Amanda as they carried on.

"How do you know them?" asked Leah with a puzzled look.

"I met them at the airport when I was collecting my luggage. She thought my bag was hers until I showed her the tag."

"You can't trust that sort," said Leah as she surveyed the back of the teenage girl sporting a short leather skirt, tattooed ankle and pink Mohawk. "They're just a bunch of wasters."

"They're OK. She's certainly friendly and even remembered my name."

"Well, you never know." Leah shook her head. "You are a bit too trusting if I recall."

When they arrived on the island later that afternoon, Leah's dad treated them to a delicious fish and chip dinner. Amanda laughed as she read out the menu, "Mushy peas – yuk. Toad in the hole? Spotted dick? That can't be real! I think I'll stick with fish and chips, thank you."

After dinner they walked down the cobblestone streets of Cowes, passing a shop with interesting used books in the window.

"Can we please stop and have a look in here?" asked Amanda.

"It's only books." Leah kept walking.

"But I love books and these look way cool."

"Why don't you girls stop in here, while I visit the shop next door to purchase some fittings for the boat."

Amanda was in her element. The dusty old store had books piled up right to the ceiling. The shelves looked like they would topple over from the weight of the volumes. The many stacks on the floor leaned to the left and to the right. The place smelled like stale, well-worn novels.

Amanda loved books so much and had a nice collection. If there was ever a fire in her house, she would throw her books out first before she jumped out of the window. Fortunately, her bedroom was on the ground floor.

Leah browsed in the romance section. Amanda drifted to a vintage section where her eyes lighted upon a copy of *Vicky and Alice*. Her great aunt Amelia had a series of these delightful books about two Victorian sisters. She would let Amanda read them when she visited. But, she hadn't seen this one before, *Vicky and Alice at the Seashore*. Amanda laughed at the picture of the girls in bathing suits that covered most of their bodies.

The price, written in pencil, was three pounds.

"I found a book I want to buy. It's a real gem!"

Leah wasn't as excited about it, but smiled politely. She had a fashion magazine in her hand. "I think I'll get this."

They gave their money to a man reading at a desk in the middle of the room. He was as dishevelled as the rest of the store, with unkempt grey hair and round glasses that sat at the end of his nose. A large, snoring tabby cat took over the only part of the desk not piled high with books and papers.

"Don't mind Rupert," said the gentleman. "He just likes to be around books. He'll do you no harm."

"A good purchase," he said as he rang in the *Vicky and Alice* book. "These are hard to come by these days." He almost smiled at Amanda.

chapter 3

The bed and breakfast, a cool old place, looked like the houses described in the *Vicky and Alice* books.

"How do I flush the toilet?" asked Amanda.

"Just pull the chain, silly," shouted Leah from their bedroom.

Amanda looked around. The only chain hung from a porcelain box high up on the wall. She gave it a tug. The toilet flushed. 'Amazing!' she thought.

Breakfast came on a huge plate: bacon, sausages, eggs, fried potatoes, mushrooms, fried tomatoes and baked beans. Amanda took a piece of unbuttered toast from a silver rack. She placed a square of butter in the middle and tried to spread it. The butter refused to move over the cold, darkened piece of bread which eventually broke in half. She decided to eat it without butter and dunked it in the soft egg yolk.

"Where are we going today?"

"I need to work on the boat," said Mr. Anderson. "I can drop you off at Osborne House for the morning. Mrs. Anderson thought it would be fun to explore."

"Oh, droll. I went there on a school trip once. It was boring." Leah rolled her eyes.

"What is it?" asked Amanda.

"It was the summer vacation house of Queen Victoria and her family. They have some very nice displays there now, and I know you would enjoy it Amanda. You could have tea there and I will pick you up after lunch," said Mr. Anderson.

"Well, at least the gardens are nice there. We could take a stroll around and talk, I guess. There isn't much else to do here anyway." Leah winked at Amanda.

Leah's dad dropped the girls off at the entrance of a large house.

"How could this be a summer vacation home?" Osborne House looked like a palace to Amanda.

A large wild boar greeted the girls on one side of the front door and a huge mastiff dog stood on the other side. Luckily, they were made of stone. Once inside, Amanda was amazed at how elegant and magnificent the house appeared. The walls covered in paintings, and the hallways lined with bronze sculptures, made it feel more like a museum than a home.

"Pretty posh, isn't it?" said Leah.

A painting of a family covered one entire wall in what seemed like the dining room. "Is this them? The royal family?" asked Amanda.

A woman wearing a crown, an elegant gentleman, three pretty little girls in frilly dresses, a young boy in a sailor suit, and a baby made up the painting.

"Yes, that's Queen Victoria, Prince Albert and five of their nine children," replied Leah.

"Nine children! What a large family. I would love to have all those brothers and sisters."

"Not me," replied Leah. "They'd just be a nuisance."

Amanda looked at the names under the painting. The three little girls were called Victoria, Alice and Helena.

"Let's check out the nursery, it might be more interesting than this." Leah started up a set of marble stairs.

The nursery seemed much cosier than the rest of the house. The furniture, still fancy but in smaller proportions, looked adorable. An old music box with a medieval castle scene, sat on a table. When Amanda turned the handle, the figures began to move. A knight on a horse pranced over the drawbridge, and a princess appeared on a balcony.

"This is so awesome," remarked Amanda.

A dollhouse and a rocking horse stood in another corner beside two cribs and a small bed. A bookshelf lined another wall. Amanda could not resist glancing through the well worn novels. She spotted a row of *Vicky and Alice* books. 'I can't believe it.' Amanda didn't know there were so many of them; twenty-two in all. She ran her eyes down the line of books to see which ones she had read. *Vicky and Alice at the Seashore* was there, but – 'wait a minute – number 14 is missing.' A small gap appeared where it should have been.

Leah looked out the window. "Come and see the garden from here, Amanda. It's a lovely view. We really should go for a walk in it."

Amanda joined her friend and agreed that the children certainly had a great view from their bedroom window. They could even see the sea.

"Hey, aren't those the teenagers you know? The ones who said hello to you on the ferry."

A girl with a bright pink Mohawk and a boy in an England T-shirt ran in and out of the shrubs and statues as if running away from someone.

"Yes, that's them all right, and it looks like she has a book in her hand. How fast can we get to the garden?" Amanda looked around for a door.

chapter 4

"This way." Leah pointed to a set of back stairs leading to a door. The girls opened the door and found themselves on a balcony overlooking the garden.

"They're over there by the fountain." Amanda started down another set of stairs.

"Hey – you, stop!" Amanda shouted as she ran past the stone fountain surrounded by red and yellow tulips. The teenagers slipped out of sight behind a hedge. Amanda passed a large, carved, black dog, a row of bird baths and a granite bench. She narrowed her eyes but couldn't see them anymore. Leah ran up beside her.

"Wowza, Amanda. You sure were running fast. What is it?"

"I think they stole a book out of the nursery. A *Vicky and Alice* book is missing. Where could they have gone?"

"I told you they were wasters. I can't see them

anywhere." Leah scanned the grounds.

"That makes me so angry. Why would anyone want to steal a *Vicky and Alice* book?" Amanda shook her head.

Leah put her arm around her friend. "Let's have a cup of tea. I don't think there is anything we can do about it."

The girls walked through the gardens and back to the terrace teahouse.

Leah ordered tea for two. The tea came in a large china pot painted with pink roses just like the ones growing in the garden around them. The waitress brought a three tiered, china serving platter filled with mini cakes, scones and dainty sandwiches.

"Oh dear, I can't decide what to eat first, it all looks so good." Amanda soon forgot about the missing book and the teenagers.

"Have one of these." Leah took a small scone, split it in two and spread what looked like cream cheese over each side. She placed a spoonful of strawberry jam in the centre. She gave one half to Amanda.

Amanda took a bite. "OMG! That has to be the best thing I have ever tasted. I like your cream cheese. It's sweeter than what we have at home."

"It's not cream cheese silly, it's clotted cream from Devon. You're right though, it is good." Leah reached for another scone.

After the girls had their fill of mini sandwiches, bite-sized cakes and more scones they sat back and viewed the scene.

"It would have been fun to grow up here, don't you think," said Amanda as she admired the carved birds sitting on the stone wall surrounding the terrace.

"Oh, I don't know. I think it would have been boring," replied Leah. "There are no shops or cinemas or anything around here."

"Should we tell anyone what we saw?" asked Amanda.

Leah sighed, "I don't think we should get involved. If those kids stole the book, they will get caught soon enough. Dad should be waiting at the front any minute now. Have you seen enough?"

"Yeah, I guess so." There had to be something more to the missing novel but Amanda had no idea what.

Later that evening, back in Cowes, Mr. Anderson needed to go to the boat supply store again.

"Let's go back to the bookstore," suggested Amanda.

"Sure, I guess there's nothing else to do." Leah led the way.

The bell tinkled as they opened the door. Rupert, still sleeping on the desk in the middle of the room, as if he had never left, lifted his head to look at them with one eye. The elderly gentleman came out from a back room, arms loaded with books. He looked as if he would topple over with the weight of them.

"Here, let me help you." Amanda rushed over to take some books from him. "Where would you like these?" She looked around for an empty space.

"Just put them on the floor over there." He pointed with his chin.

"Thank you, luv. Can I help you find something?" the man asked as he put the rest of the books down on the floor in front of the desk.

"Do you have any more *Vicky and Alice* books?"

"Sorry, no. They are hard to come by these days. You were lucky to get the one you did for such a good price. Soon they will be worth quite a few pounds."

"I saw a complete set at Osborne House today. Well, almost complete. Number 14 was missing."

The old man looked up in alarm. "Missing, you say. Oh my. That is not good. Who would do such a thing as steal from a museum?"

"Well, we s–"

"We have no idea sir," interrupted Leah as she gave Amanda a warning glance. "I'm sure they will soon catch the thieves."

Just then Rupert stretched his legs, flexed his claws and produced a quiet meow. He sat up, looked around, jumped off the desk, ran around the stack of books and disappeared.

Amanda wondered if Rupert knew something they didn't.

chapter 5

"**I** think we should have told the man about what we saw," said Amanda after they left the bookstore, holding onto the two books she had just purchased.

"We don't know for sure if those kids stole the book. You just think you saw a book in that girl's hand. You don't want to mess with their sort, Amanda." Leah tried to look serious.

"What sort would that be then, miss?"

Amanda and Leah stopped and turned around. The girl with the pink Mohawk stood right behind them, holding the cat from the bookstore.

"What are you doing with Rupert? You better not hurt him. And why did you steal the book from the nursery at Osborne House?" Amanda walked up to the girl and tried to take Rupert out of her hands.

"Hold on, Amanda from Canada." With a firm grip on the cat, the girl stepped back.

Just then the boy with the tattoos came around

the corner. "Wot's goin' on?"

The girl pointed her finger at Amanda. "She's accusing me of catnapping and stealing a book."

The boy laughed out loud. "Don't be daft. Rylee here'd never hurt a cat and as far as stealin' a book, well - she can't actually read."

"Liam! I can too read. I just wouldn't steal a book." She punched him on the shoulder. Rupert squirmed in her arms.

Leah looked up and down the empty, shadowy street. "Amanda, let's just go."

Amanda ignored her. "So, what were you doing hiding in the bushes at Osborne House then? It looked like you had a book in your hand."

"Tell her, Liam."

"By all means. Ya see, we weren't hidin' in the bushes. We were havin' a little picnic. And we brought along a book of poetry to read. Didn't we, Rylee?"

"Oh, Liam, stop messing about and just tell her the truth." Rupert pushed her arm away with his front paws and jumped down. He ran off into the darkness.

"Now look, you made him run off again."

"He'll just go back to Uncle Charlie's bookstore. He'll be all right," said Liam.

"The bookstore belongs to your Uncle?" Amanda

looked surprised.

"Yeh, he's had it for years. He should retire but he won't, so Mum has me come over and help him on occasion. This is my girlfriend, Rylee. She helps out, sometimes. We just like to hang out at the big house, see how the rich folk used to live, like. The security guards don't much care for us. Guess 'cause of how we look. They think we're wasters." He looked right at Leah and winked. She blushed.

"Look, we didn't steal no book. Rylee had a book with her from the book shop to read on the bus. We can get all the books we want from Uncle Charlie; why'd we steal one? D'you wanna come for a soda?'

"Sure," said Amanda.

"Sorry, we have to meet my dad in a couple of minutes," said Leah at the same time.

"Well then, maybe another time." Liam shrugged. He and Rylee turned to walk back toward the book-store.

"Are you completely mental?" seethed Leah. "They could be dangerous or get us involved in some weird book stealing scam."

"They seem OK to me. Besides Liam is the nephew of the bookstore owner. He can't be that bad."

"I'm not sure I actually believe them. Look, here's Dad. I'm starved."

Back at the bed and breakfast, Amanda pulled out

the books she had purchased at the bookstore. One was about cats. She loved cats and would have liked one as a pet, but her mom was allergic. She leafed through the book and stopped at a page with a picture of a grey and black striped, long-haired tabby with tufts at the top of his ears and a ruff around his neck.

"Look at this, Leah. Doesn't this look just like Rupert?"

"I guess so. He is big and fluffy like Rupert."

"It says here they are called Maine Coon cats; they are extremely friendly and cuddly, loyal like dogs and love to be around people. They are also more intelligent than regular cats and easy to train."

"That's probably why he likes living in a bookstore." Leah peered over Amanda's shoulder. "It also says they are known to be quite mischievous when bored and can use their front paws for many things. I noticed how he got out of that girl's grasp by pushing her arm with his front paws. Rupert - the smart, dexterous bookstore cat."

"What do you mean, dexterous?"

"You're the bookish one. I would have thought you'd know." Leah grinned.

"Have you ever had a cat, Leah?"

"Yeh, once when I was only little. She died and I was sad. Her name was Priscilla. We never got another one because we started moving around with dad's work."

The girls sat on the edge of the bed looking through the book to see if they could find one that looked like Leah's cat. They forgot all about the missing book for the time being.

chapter 6

A sharp knock on the door disturbed Amanda's dream. "Wake up girls. It's almost time to go. Look lively."

"Ooh – Dad, do we have to get up so early?" moaned Leah.

"If Amanda still wants to go for a sailboat ride, you do."

"Yes. Yes, I do." Amanda pushed aside the warm covers and swung her legs out of the bed.

"Really, Amanda, why do you want to go out on the silly sailboat?"

"Because I've never been on one before. Remember, I live in the middle of the Canadian prairies where there is no large body of water and no sailboats. This would be a dream come true for me."

"All right then." Leah gave a big stretch and smiled. "The things I do for you, honestly. We'll be down in a minute, Dad."

The early morning, thirty minute drive to the

dock delighted Amanda. They passed thatched roofed cottages with giant rhododendron bushes in the yards and purple wisteria dangling from the eaves. She expected to see elves running around the bright green lawns and hiding under the toadstools.

They pulled into a small village and parked the car near a murky canal where many boats were lined up, patiently waiting to make their way out to the sea. The cool air smelled salty and fishy.

Mr. Anderson handed Leah some money and said, "You two should get something to eat while I fit the new piece of equipment. It should only take me an hour and then we can go out." He looked up at the darkening sky. "If the weather doesn't turn bad, that is."

Amanda felt a chill breeze; she zipped up her hoodie as they started down an old street. They passed an ancient looking building with a green and white sign swinging from a hook. Amanda stopped to read the sign:

GOD'S PROVIDENCE HOUSE 1701

"Leah, can you believe this building has been around since 1701?"

"Yeah, so what. That's not even that old." Leah shrugged her shoulders.

"Well it sure seems old to me. Where I come from

nothing is more than a hundred years old. If these walls could talk, I bet they would have some great stories to tell."

"This looks like a good place to get some breakfast." Leah stopped in front of a bakery with mouth watering pastries in the window. The warm smell of fresh baking and coffee greeted them as they entered the cozy, crowded shop.

While Amanda enjoyed her hot chocolate and blueberry muffin, she checked out the other customers. Two old guys with fishing gear sat in a corner discussing the weather. A young couple held hands as they sipped their tea and looked into each others eyes. 'I bet they're newlyweds,' thought Amanda. Surrounded by shopping bags overflowing with vegetables, bread, pastries and books, a woman with grey hair and round glasses sat reading a book. She looked at her watch, closed her book and put it in one of the bags, which fell over causing other books to tumble out. Amanda rushed over to help her.

"No! It's OK. I've got it." The woman picked up the scattered books and shoved them in a bag. Amanda thought she glimpsed a *Vicky and Alice* book amongst the assortment. The woman struggled out of the bakery with her bulging bags hitting the backs of her legs.

"That's strange," said Amanda when she came

back to the table. "I'm sure she had a *Vicky and Alice* book in there she didn't want me to see."

"You sure do have an active imagination, Amanda. Let's go if you're finished."

The girls passed an old church just as the bells began to chime. Amazed at the view of the stone exterior, Amanda stared up at a carved angel smiling down at her from a window while carvings of heads perched on corners. Amanda wondered who they represented.

She glanced at a doorway. There stood the woman from the bakery. Nervously, the woman looked both ways as if expecting someone. Amanda wanted to ask her about the book, but thought better of it as Leah had kept walking and was quite a ways ahead.

Amanda caught up to Leah as she neared the graveyard beside the church.

"Can we stop and look at the gravestones?" asked Amanda.

"What? Why do you want to look at gravestones?"

"I love looking at the dates and inscriptions. I bet there are some real old ones here."

Leah looked at her and shook her head. "You never cease to amaze me. I figured you were curious and bookish but now I find you're morbid too."

Tombstones were scattered about, most of them bent forward or backward. Some large and ornate while others small and plain. Most of the writing was worn off, but Amanda found one that read *Amelia Burns 1792 – 1804*. She felt a chill run through her body when she realized the person was her age when she died. She couldn't help wonder what the young girl died of.

The peaceful cemetery smelt of freshly mown grass. Among the many large trees, a huge weeping willow stood in a corner providing protection for the dead.

Leah shouted to Amanda, "Over here, you'll want to see these."

Leah stood in a field of daisies. When Amanda joined her she discovered even older gravestones hidden amongst the tall grass and flowers. The writing was completely worn off and chunks had fallen away from the stones. She could barely read a date of sixteen something on one marker. Amanda had never seen such old tombstones. She shivered. The sun had gone behind an ominous cloud.

Amanda felt like she was being watched. 'It must be being around all these dead people,' she thought.

Then she saw some movement in the trees. "Leah, did you see that?"

"What?"

"Someone's in the trees watching us."

"There goes that imagination again. I better get

you out of here before you start to spook me too."
Leah grabbed Amanda by the arm and then let out
a scream as a large cat ran in front, almost tripping
them, and disappeared behind a gravestone.

A dishevelled older man emerged from behind
the willow tree flailing his arms and shouting, "Rupert, come back here this instant."

chapter 7

"It's Uncle Charlie from the bookstore. What's he doing here?" asked a shocked Amanda as they watched the old man chase Rupert around old gravestones and disappear down the street. "He must have been hiding behind that tree all the time. Do you think he was spying on us?"

Leah shook her head. "Perhaps he was waiting for someone. Who knows? All I know, it's none of our affair."

Amanda stared at the huge willow tree. "I think he left something behind." She walked over to investigate. "Leah, look at this – a bag of books. Now why would he be hiding behind a tree, in a grave-yard – with a bag of books? This is all too weird."

"Like I said, it's none of our concern. We must be getting back to the boat." Leah turned toward the dock.

Amanda picked up the bag of books and followed her.

When they got to the boat, Leah noticed the bag in Amanda's hand, "What are you planning to do with those?"

"We need to get them back to Uncle Charlie when we return to Cowes. Don't we?"

"You should have just left them, Amanda. Dad, can we have the keys to the car so we can put something in the boot before we go for a sail?"

"Go ahead, love. It's open," shouted Mr. Anderson from inside the boat. "We're almost ready to set sail. Make sure you put on your life jackets before coming aboard."

After donning the lifejackets, the girls boarded the boat called *Shelagh*. "That is so cool you named the boat after your wife, Mr. Anderson. I like the way it's spelled too. I'm used to the name being spelled S-h-e-i-l-a."

"It's the old Gaelic spelling. It wouldn't have done to name the boat after a former girlfriend, would it?" Leah's dad winked as he held out his hand to help Amanda onto the boat. "Welcome aboard, have a look around."

Amanda followed Leah down short wooden stairs into a small room that looked like a mini kitchen.

"This is the galley," reported Leah, "and this is the head."

"Wow, that's the smallest bathroom I have ever

seen. It's so cute."

"Well, I wouldn't exactly call it that. Here are the instructions if you need to use the toilet. Listen carefully because Dad gets awful angry if we mess up the toilet. First fill it with water by pushing this lever to the left." Leah demonstrated. "Then when you are finished, push the lever to the right to flush it. And never, ever, throw tissue in the toilet, put it in the basket. Did you get that?"

"Sure, left to fill with water, right to flush and no tissue in the toilet." Amanda hoped she didn't have to use it in case she messed up. She didn't want to make Mr. Anderson angry after he had been so kind to her. She had trouble imagining him angry though.

"OK girls, we're almost ready. Put the tea kettle in the sink and make sure there's nothing loose. We don't want things to go flying." Mr. Anderson studied a large map while listening to a radio that crackled, making it hard to understand. "Good, we are at 16 knots - that's a good wind speed. Sounds like the weather should hold out."

"What's 16 knots and what do all those swirly lines and arrows mean on the map? Could we get lost in the ocean?"

Leah's dad scratched his head, "Well, 16 knots is the speed we will be going. Just like cars go miles per hour, or, I guess you would say kilometres per hour. 16 knots would be equivalent to 30 kilometres per hour. The map is called a chart and it just keeps us on track. There is no danger of us getting lost this close to land so don't worry, Amanda. Your Captain knows what he's doing." Mr. Anderson picked up a pair of binoculars and a hand held radio. "All set, crew? Let's go."

"You can help me take the covers off the sails," said Leah as she jumped on top of the boat. Together the girls unsnapped the covers and put them safely away. Then Leah pulled up large rubber cylinders hanging from the side of the boat as her dad started the engine. She untied a rope that kept the boat tied to the dock and shouted, "All clear!" as they pulled away. Leah impressed Amanda with how she knew her way around a sailboat.

Leah handed Amanda one of the rubber tubes and said, "Could you please put this fender behind your seat." Amanda made a note to remember they were called fenders, kind of like fenders on a car.

Amanda couldn't believe she was actually on a sailboat as they left the dock and went through a narrow opening piled high with rocks on each side. The rocks were covered with seagulls as if hired to watch the boats come in and out. Suddenly, they were out in open water. The wind caught Amanda's hair and whipped it around. The boat lurched. It felt like she was riding a camel again.

Mr. Anderson put on a pair of gloves without fingers and took the straps off the mainsail. He hit a button and the sail went up, flapping around like a frightened bird. When the sail filled with wind, it looked like a large, white pillow. He turned a lever on a round metal post circled with rope and the tightly rolled up, front sail unfurled. With two sails up, they glided out into the ocean.

Soon Amanda's tummy got used to bobbing up and down with the boat. She watched the foamy, white tipped waves lap along the sides of the *Shelagh*. She listened to the creaking sounds of the sails as they did their job moving the boat forward. 'This is how it must have been for the ancient explorers as they crossed the ocean looking for new lands,' she thought.

The boat tilted over and Amanda slid all the way over to the other side. A couple of huge waves came up over the boat soaking her.

Leah laughed. "So, how do you like sailing now?"

"It's fun," laughed Amanda as she wiped the water off her glasses. She licked her lips and tasted the salty water.

Mr. Anderson stood behind a large wheel in the centre of the boat. "Would you like to steer, Amanda?"

"Gosh, could I?"

"Sure. Here you go. Just turn it a little to the left and a bit to the right. There, you are doing it."

Amanda held onto the huge wheel and concentrated on what she was doing. "OMG, this is so exciting. I never thought I would be steering a boat."

The sky darkened. Leah's dad said, "We had better turn back. I don't like the look of those clouds. It could get nasty out here. We're going to tack now so watch out for the boom."

"What? What is tack? What is boom?" asked a puzzled Amanda.

"When we tack, we change the direction of the sails and the boom is this pole coming toward you – duck!"

Amanda looked up and saw a large metal pole coming right across the boat. It was no where near her head, but she ducked anyway. Leah laughed.

It got a lot colder, wetter and windier on the way back. The boat rocked harder and sometimes leaned far to one side. Amanda wondered if boats ever went all the way over but didn't want to ask. By the time they were back at the dock and tied up it started to rain.

"Looks like we just got back in time. How was that, Amanda?" asked Mr. Anderson.

"It was super cool. Thanks a bunch. I can't wait to tell the kids back home."

Later that night, warm and safe in their room at the B & B, Amanda looked through the books in the bag left behind by Uncle Charlie. They were very old books and smelled musty. None of them seemed remotely interesting to her except for a *Vicky and Alice* book at the bottom of the bag. It wasn't the missing number fourteen, but neither was it one she had seen before. She had a suspicious feeling something weird was going on with those books.

chapter 8

"**M**r. Anderson, can we please stop at the bookstore once more before we catch the ferry?" asked Amanda as she put hot sauce on her scrambled eggs.

"Of course, luv. I need to stop at the boat supply store for one more thing anyway."

"Thanks so much." Amanda liked that he called her "love". It made her feel like part of the family.

Leah screwed up her nose. "How can you eat your eggs with hot sauce?"

"I just like spicy things, that's all. Eggs are kind of boring otherwise." Amanda added more sauce.

When they arrived at the bookstore, Liam was hanging the OPEN sign.

"Where is your Uncle Charlie?" Amanda put the bag of books on the counter and looked around. "And where is Rupert?"

"Dunno. They went out yesterday and I haven't seen hide nor hair of either one of 'em. Now I have to look after the store. Was planning to go to the beach, but there you have it." He looked a bit grumpy. "Daft old man. I told me mum he's losing it you know. Liam looked at the bag on the counter. "What's this then?"

"Yesterday, we saw your Uncle Charlie in the graveyard at Newport and he was hiding behind a tree and when he went to catch Rupert who was running away, he left this bag of books behind." Amanda stopped to catch her breath.

"Hold on. Are you telling me the old duffer was in Newport, hiding behind a tree, in a graveyard?" Liam looked at Leah. "Does your friend always spin yarns like this?"

Leah sighed, "I am afraid what she says is true. I saw him too and Rupert gave us a huge scare. Can we just leave the books here for your uncle? We're about to leave for the ferry."

"Guess so." Liam scratched his head. "But I don't know what he'd be doing in Newport with a bag of books?" He peered in the bag and pulled out a couple of books. "Hello, what have we here? Aren't these the ones Uncle Charlie said went missing from the store the other day? He was all upset 'cause he said they were rare and worth a pretty penny. This just don't figure."

"We hope he returns soon and is OK. We have

to go – now." Leah grabbed Amanda's arm. "Dad's waiting."

All the way back on the ferry Amanda kept thinking about Uncle Charlie, the bag of books, and the missing *Vicky and Alice* book from Osborne House. It just didn't add up. As they were about to go the car, she thought she saw the lady from the bakery. 'Did she have something to do with all this'?

><

The next morning, Leah asked her mom if they could go into London to do some shopping.

"Not today, dear. I have to look in on old Mrs. Clancy. She is poorly and I said I would check in on her and bring her some groceries. How about I drop you off at Hampton Court? Amanda would love it there and you always like exploring the maze."

"I would have really rather gone shopping and shown Amanda the London fashions."

"Don't worry. We will do that another day."

"What is Hampton Court?" asked Amanda.

"It was one of Henry VIII's homes," replied Mrs. Anderson.

"Henry VIII? The guy with all the wives? I've read about him. You bet I would love to visit his house."

"That's settled then. I will drop you off at Hampton Court and pick you up in a couple of hours. Then we can go for a nice tea."

"With those wonderful scones, Devon cream, and strawberry jam?" Amanda grinned. "This day sounds better all the time."

chapter 9

"**W**OW! Now that's what I call a palace." Amanda stared in amazement at the massive, pink brick building in front of her. "I have never seen anything so huge and magnificent. How could anyone live here? You would get lost everyday. Where do we start?"

"You are too funny, Amanda." Leah grabbed her hand and pulled her through a large archway into a courtyard. "Just stick with me and you won't get lost."

A woman in a long, wine coloured dress, with a white ruffled collar that made her look like she had no neck, approached the girls. She handed them a map. "Here is a guide for you young ladies. Just follow the numbers and you'll be all right."

Men wearing floppy berets, white tights, and what looked like knee length dresses, offered to show them around and answer any questions.

"Are those guys wearing dresses?" asked Amanda.

"That's what men wore in the fourteenth century. I think they were called tunics."

"Oh - this should be fun!" squealed Amanda as they entered a marble hallway.

The girls wandered through large rooms and long hallways filled with ornate old furniture, life-sized statues and tapestries that covered entire walls.

Leah yawned, "Let's go down to the kitchen, it might be more interesting."

"But it's not the next stop," explained Amanda as she studied the map.

"We don't have to follow the silly old map exactly."

Leah started walking down a set of stone stairs that led to a dimly lit room in stark contrast to the rooms upstairs. Fireplaces lined the whitewashed walls. Hanging metal pots waited to serve the many guests that would have been entertained in the days of Henry VIII. Pewter plates, mugs and bowls were stacked on long tables. Amanda backed away from a huge, hairy, black pig lying on a wooden table.

"Yuk – what's that?"

"It's a wild boar. Popular medieval feast fare. Usually served with an apple in its ugly mouth."

Amanda screamed. Something furry ran across her feet.

"O-M-G – was, was that a rat?"

"I hardly think so. Tourists wouldn't come here if

they let rats run around," reassured Leah.

"I need to get out of here – now." Amanda shook from head to toe, cemented to the spot.

Beside a fireplace, a small door stood ajar. Leah opened it further. "This leads to a small hallway. It should get us out quickly." She pulled Amanda behind her, dragging her like a dead cat.

Suddenly the door shut behind them, leaving them in darkness. Two green eyes glowed in a corner.

"OMG, OMG, OMG." Amanda stammered.

"Just hang on to me. I'll get us out of here ASAP." Leah held on to Amanda with one hand. "I'll feel my way along the wall. Here, I think this is a door handle." Leah tugged at the handle and they stepped into bright sunshine, surrounded by a hedgerow. A large, grey fluffy cat ran out the door and disappeared into the maze.

Amanda blinked her eyes to get used to the sun. "Was that? Could it possibly be..."

"Don't be silly. Rupert is on the Isle of Wight."

"We don't know that for sure. Last thing we heard, Rupert was missing."

Amanda ran after the cat leaving Leah with no choice but to follow. They ran up and down the maze, around many corners, feeling they were going in circles. Sometimes they caught glimpses of the cat, but never got close enough to catch him. At last they stopped to catch their breath.

"Well, how do we get out of here?" asked Leah. "Does your magic guide map show us?"

Amanda looked around. "Oh no, I must have dropped it."

They walked for what seemed like miles, always hitting dead ends. They could hear voices at times but never ever saw anyone.

"This is spooky. What if we never find our way out?" Amanda sounded worried.

They turned yet another corner and there in front of them was the grey haired woman from the bakery in Newport. Rupert struggled in her arms.

"What are you doing here, with Rupert?" asked Leah.

Rupert's hair stuck up at all angles. His eyes as big as frisbees. He pushed the woman's hands away with his massive paws, jumped out of her grasp and disappeared through the hedge. The girls attempted to follow him and noticed a gap in the hedge. They looked back; the woman was gone.

"Let's see if we can get through this hole," suggested Amanda.

The hedge scratched their arms and snagged their hair as they squeezed through the tight opening. Once through, they found themselves outside the maze.

Amanda breathed a sigh of relief, "Well, at least we're out of there."

Rupert appeared from around a corner and approached the girls. He rubbed up against Leah's leg. She bent down to stroke him. "What is it, mate? What are you doing here, so far from home?"

Leah looked at Amanda, "I think he's trying to tell us something."

Rupert ran to the corner and back again. He looked up at Leah with big, pleading eyes. "OK, we had better follow you."

They rounded the corner and there on the ground, with a nasty gash on his forehead, lay Uncle Charlie. He wasn't moving. Rupert stood beside him like a palace guard.

chapter 10

"Uncle Charlie, Uncle Charlie, are you all right?" Amanda patted his shoulder. She put her ear to his mouth and felt a whiff of warm air. "He's breathing at least."

Leah saw the top of a floppy beret on the other side of a hedge. "Help! Over here! We need some help over here."

Within seconds a man appeared and whipped out his cell phone. "Do you know this man?" he asked the girls.

"Not really," said Leah at the same time as Amanda said, "He's Uncle Charlie from the bookstore on the Isle of Wight."

"I'm sorry, do you know him or don't you?" asked the puzzled guide.

"We have been to his bookstore," explained Leah. "But we don't really know him."

"The ambulance will be here in a minute. Perhaps you two should wait here."

"Excuse me, sir. May I borrow your mobile to make a quick call to my mother? She'll be waiting at the gate."

"Of course, luv." The guide handed her his cell phone.

The ambulance and Mrs. Anderson arrived at the same time, followed by a police officer.

"Are you two all right?" asked a concerned Mrs. Anderson.

"Yes, we got lost in the maze and couldn't find our way out. Then we found Rupert with a weird lady and he led us to Uncle Charlie who was lying on the ground with a big gash on his head."

"Slow down, Amanda," said Mrs. Anderson. "Who is Rupert? I didn't know you had an Uncle Charlie in England."

"Well, he's not my Uncle Charlie, he's Liam's. Rupert is his cat who is very smart. He knew Uncle Charlie was hurt and led us to him, just like a dog would."

Mrs. Anderson still looked confused.

They put Uncle Charlie on a stretcher and took him away in an ambulance. The police officer approached the girls. "What do you know about this, young ladies?"

"We came out of the maze and the cat, Rupert, led us to the man from the bookstore in Cowes," explained Leah.

The police officer pulled out a small notebook from his pocket. "Was he passed out when you came upon him?"

"Yes, sir. We thought he might be dead."

"Did you see anything odd or suspicious?"

"Not really - except a strange lady in the maze. She tried to hold onto Rupert, but he got away. Maybe she didn't want us to find the man."

Amanda was impressed with how Leah explained things so clearly and precisely.

The police officer asked a few more questions, like how they knew Uncle Charlie. He took a description of the lady and wrote down their names and phone number in case he needed to speak to them again. "What are we to do about this cat then?"

"Can he come home with us for now?" asked Leah.

Rupert looked up at Mrs. Anderson with appealing eyes. "I guess so," she replied.

With everyone, including Rupert, settled into the car, Leah's mom asked if they still wanted to go for high tea.

"Would I? I'm starved and a tea would be so great," said Amanda.

"I'm famished too, Mum."

Rupert barely opened one eye as he settled in for a nap.

Amanda bit into a delicious scone smothered in Devon cream and strawberry jam. "That was some maze at Hampton Court. Why did they make them like that?"

Mrs. Anderson smiled. "The one at Hampton Court is the oldest surviving hedge maze and was built as a puzzle meant to be challenging and fun for the idle people at court. I am sure there are many stories and secrets held amongst those paths and hedgerows."

"Well, it was kind of scary when we couldn't find our way out. If Rupert hadn't led us to the hole in the hedge, we might still be in there."

"I hope Rupert's okay in the car, Mum."

"We left the window open a little, and he seemed to be sound asleep. I am sure he will be fine. I think we still have the sleeping basket and food bowl from Priscilla that he can use. It will be nice to have a cat in the house again, even if for just a while." Mrs. Anderson wiped Devon cream off her lip with a white linen napkin.

chapter 11

The next morning, Leah's mom served breakfast in the sunny back garden where Amanda and Leah watched Rupert play with a ball. He caught it with his paws and batted it back and forth. He suddenly stopped playing and sat on his back legs staring at the hedge, the tuffs on his ears sticking straight up.

"What's up with Rupert?" asked Leah.

"What is that?" shouted Amanda as a prickly looking animal emerged from under the hedge. Covered in bristles, it had a long snout like a baby pig. "Is it a small porcupine?"

"Oh, that. It's just a hedgehog. They're everywhere and eat the bugs in the garden."

At that moment, the small animal rolled up into a prickly ball. Rupert sat and stared at it, ready to pounce and bat it around.

"No! Rupert, don't hurt him," shouted Leah.

Rupert didn't move.

"Does it hurt to touch them?" asked Amanda.

"Oh, no. Some people keep them as pets. They roll up like that to protect themselves." Leah walked over to the hedge and picked up the frightened animal. She brought it over to Amanda who reached out and touched it.

"It feels kind of like a hairbrush, not really prickly but bristly. He's actually quite cute."

Leah turned the hedgehog over. "Feel his tummy."

Amanda stroked the white fur. "It's very soft and fluffy. I've never ever seen a hedgehog before. I thought they were just in fairy tales, not real animals at all."

Leah put the hedgehog back under the hedge. "Oh, they are real all right. They usually only come out in the evening."

"Can we go shopping today, Mum?" she asked when Mrs. Anderson came out to clear away the plates.

"Sure, we can take the train into town. Can you be ready in forty-five minutes?"

They reached downtown London after a twenty minute train ride and were soon in front of a huge fancy building that covered an entire block. Amanda noticed many flags flying above green awnings and asked, "Is this another palace?"

Just then, a tall young man wearing a green tuxedo jacket with gold trim and a green top hat smiled and said, "Welcome to Harrods," as he opened the big glass doors.

Amanda was speechless as she viewed the dazzling sight before her. Everything sparkled, the chandeliers, the gold covered walls, the brightly lit display cases filled with jewelry, watches, perfumes, and scarves.

When she finally caught her breath she said, "I think this place is too expensive for me."

"It is fun to look at all the lovely things," said Mrs. Anderson as she held on to Amanda's hand. "Let's go upstairs to the souvenir section. There might be something there for you."

As they rode up the escalator, Amanda looked up and saw the ceiling painted with pictures. They walked past gold Egyptian pillars and even a sphinx. It seemed more like a museum than a department store, except everyone carried green plastic bags the same colour as the awnings and the doorman's suit. Obviously, they were there to shop.

Mrs. Anderson led them to an area with souvenir items. In the middle sat an oversized teddy bear dressed in a scarlet-red tunic, trimmed in gold and black with a huge white ruff around his neck and a gold crown embroidered on his chest. On his head, sat a black round hat trimmed with red, white and blue flowers.

"He is so cute." Amanda ran her hand over his plush foot.

"Here's one for you, for only £8.95," said Leah as she held up a smaller version.

"A Beefeater bear would be a wonderful souvenir for you to take home Amanda," said Leah's mother.

"Why are they called Beefeaters?"

"They guard the Tower of London and have done so for hundreds of years. It is said they guarded the King's food and made sure it wasn't poisoned by tasting it first. No one is sure where the name actually came from but that's one story," explained Mrs. Anderson.

Amanda bought the small bear for herself, a tin of cookies in the shape of a beefeater bear for her mother, a miniature double-decker bus for her friend and a cat tea cozy for her great aunt Amelia. The sales clerk put her purchases in one of the famous green bags which Amanda proudly carried.

They could hear an argument as they went down the escalator.

"I am sorry, Miss, but you are not allowed in Harrods dressed like that." A security guard was addressing a young girl with a bright pink Mohawk.

"I'm just lookin' for my friends. I don't wanna buy any of your naff stuff."

The security guard was polite but firm. "Mohawks are not allowed in Harrods, and we have a strict dress code. Please leave the premises now."

"I'll just be a minute. I need to find 'em, it's important."

The voice sounded very familiar. Amanda looked at Leah.

"I'll be gob-smacked. There they are!" Rylee pointed right at Amanda and Leah.

Chapter 12

Leah's face went pale. Mrs. Anderson looked puzzled.

Amanda smiled and said, "Hi Rylee. What are you doing here? Why are you looking for us?"

With her hand on Rylee's elbow, the security guard steered her toward the door and said, "Could you please carry on this conversation outside the store."

"I'm going. Don't fret."

Amanda, Leah and her mother followed.

Once outside, Rylee started to explain. "Liam was worried about his Uncle Charlie because he'd not been back home for a couple of days now and the cat was gone too. He called the police. They said a man his age and description had been hit on the head and was in hospital in London. They said two girls who knew him, reported it. We figured it was you two. Liam sent me here to find out what's going on. I followed you to Harrods, but the snobby twits wouldn't let me in."

"Well I shouldn't think so, dressed like that," said Mrs. Anderson as she eyed the short, leather skirt and tight T-shirt. "How do you girls know each other?"

Leah, Amanda and Rylee took turns explaining how they all met and what had happened so far. Tears came to Rylee's eyes when she heard about Uncle Charlie. "He's not a bad sort, really. Who'd want to hurt a nice old man like that? I hope he'll be OK. What about Rupert? What's happened to him?"

"We have him," said Leah. "He's at my house, sleeping, I imagine."

"That's all right then." Rylee looked relieved. "Thanks. Can I hang with you for a bit?"

Leah's mom bought everyone lunch and then excused herself to look in at a dress shop next door.

"Whad'ya reckon we should do about all this?" asked Rylee.

"There's nothing we can do. It's out of our hands," replied Leah. "We can look after Rupert as long as needed, and that's all."

"We have to try and find who is behind all of this." Amanda looked directly at Rylee. "Did you take the missing *Vicky and Alice* book from Osborne House?"

"No, I didn't. Why would I do a thing like that?"

"Well, I think whoever took that book is behind Uncle Charlie's odd behaviour and now his injury."

Rylee took a folded piece of paper from her denim handbag. "Liam wanted me to give this to you."

Amanda took the paper and unfolded it.

MEET ME AT THE TOWER OF LONDON ON WEDNESDAY

"What is this? Where did you get it?"

"Liam found it while cleaning off Uncle Charlie's desk yesterday. He thought it might be a clue as to what's going on."

"What day is it?" Amanda looked at Leah.

"It's Wednesday."

"Then we need to go to the Tower of London."

Just then Leah's mom appeared carrying shopping bags.

"Mrs. Anderson, I have always wanted to see the Tower of London. I've read so much about it. Is it nearby? Could we see it today?'

Leah glared at Amanda.

"Of course, luv. It would be a lovely way to spend the afternoon. We haven't been for ages."

They were greeted at the gates of the tower by a friendly Beefeater, dressed just like the teddy bear. Leah took a picture of Amanda beside him. Then Mrs. Anderson took a picture of all three girls with him.

"At least they let me in here." Rylee tugged at her skirt to bring it down a bit.

"You girls look around the tower while I go have a look at the crown jewels," said Mrs. Anderson.

"We don't even know who we are looking for or where they will be." Leah waved her hand around the vast site. The Tower of London was not one tower, but many towers clumped together.

"That's true, but we can look around and see what happens. You never know." Amanda examined the map the Beefeater had given her. "Over there is Tower Green, where Ann Boleyn was beheaded - can you believe it!"

Leah and Rylee shrugged their shoulders and followed her.

A Beefeater was explaining the famous beheadings to a tour group when a large black bird swooped down and almost sat on the Beefeater's head.

"Never mind him," said the Beefeater. "That's just Merlin, one of the seven Tower ravens. Legend says that the Tower, and England, will fall if the six resident ravens ever leave this place. We don't know if that is true, but we keep seven here all the time, just in case."

"How do you keep them from flying away? Are they kept in cages?" Amanda couldn't help asking.

"One wing is clipped to ensure they don't fly very

far. It doesn't hurt them. They are left free to fly around the grounds. They have a good life and live a lot longer than they would in the wild. One raven, called Jim Crow, lived to be forty-four years old."

"What do they eat?"

"They eat like kings. They get six ounces of raw meat every day and a biscuit soaked in blood. Once a week they get an egg."

"Where are the rest of them?" Amanda was fascinated.

"They can be seen anywhere amongst the towers. See if you can spot all of them during your visit. Their names are Hugine, Erin, Munin, Rocky, Pearl, Porshe and of course Merlin."

Rylee pointed to a ledge on a nearby roof. "See there, by that gargoyle, there's another one."

Amanda saw the bird and gasped. Behind the raven, crouched the woman from the bakery.

chapter 13

Amanda grasped Leah's hand. "We have to get into that building and see what she's doing here."

The woman inched her way around the corner of the roof.

"Do you think she left the note for Uncle Charlie?" asked Rylee.

"Perhaps. She was in the maze holding Rupert just before he led us to Uncle Charlie. She must have something to do with all this."

A sign outside the door of the building said:

BRICK TOWER ROYAL MENAGERIE

Amanda consulted her map. "This is where they kept the animals given to the Kings and Queens as gifts."

Upon entering, the girls heard the roar of lions, the trumpeting of elephants and the chatter of monkeys. A guide approached them and said, "Follow the path if you wish to see what animals were kept at the Tower from the 13th to the 19th century."

They rounded a corner and came upon a full sized lion and two lionesses. Rylee stepped back. "Me gosh, I thought they were real for a sec."

"They sure did a good job of making the sculptures look real," commented Amanda. "Look at the polar bear! It says here it was a gift from Canada to King George III. I wonder how they got him here."

"I wonder how that lady got on the roof." Leah reminded them of the reason they were there.

They didn't need to wonder long. The lady lurked behind the baboon display.

"Hey you! Are you following us?" Amanda approached her, hands on hips.

The lady stopped and looked around as if she didn't know whether to run or confront them. Finally she said in a low husky voice, "What are you doing here? Where is the old man with my books?"

"What books?" All three girls asked at the same time.

"The books he promised to sell me. He didn't show up in Newport, then he didn't show up at the maze, just his despicable cat, and now he isn't showing up here, is he?"

"What were you doing on the roof?" asked Amanda.

"To get a good view."

"Seriously, do you really think we are going to believe that?" Leah was annoyed. "It looked like you were trying to hide from someone."

The lady pushed her round glasses up her nose and glanced around. "Don't be so loud."

"Who are you running from? Who hit Uncle Charlie over the head?" Leah demanded answers.

"Quick. Hide before they see us," said the lady as she turned in the direction of a kangaroo. Leah and Rylee hid behind some zebras and Amanda slid behind a black bear as two men in black suits, looking very official, came around a corner. They surveyed the zoo, shrugged their shoulders and walked back out.

Amanda heard one man say, "She doesn't seem to be here either. Are you sure she was to meet the old guy here today?"

'Who are those guys?' thought Amanda as she peered around the bear. Then she saw the lady disappear near the crocodile pond. 'We need to talk to that woman.'

Taking a short cut, Amanda ran after her. She ducked under the rope surrounding the pond. Her flip flops slipped on the muddy edge. She felt herself sliding into the water and came face-to-face with a crocodile. For a minute she forgot it wasn't real and screamed.

The guide, Leah and Rylee came to her rescue and pulled her out of the water, sopping wet.

"Are you all right, luv?" asked the concerned guide. "You really mustn't venture inside the ropes. Didn't you see the sign?" She pointed to a large sign that said:

STAY OUTSIDE THE ROPED AREAS

"I – I'm s-so sorry. I guess I just was excited to see the crocodiles up close. I've never s-seen one before." Amanda's teeth chattered.

"We had better find Mom and get you home to dry out," said Leah.

They found Mrs. Anderson coming out of the tower that held the crown jewels.

"Oh, there you are." She waved at them. "What has happened to Amanda? Why is she all wet?" she asked as she got closer.

"Rylee pushed her into the crocodile pond." Leah winked at Amanda.

"I did so not do that." Rylee was indignant.

"I wasn't l-looking and got too close to the pond, slipped in the m-m-mud and f-f-fell in," explained a shivering Amanda.

Mrs. Anderson took a pullover out of her carrying bag and gave it to Amanda. "This jumper should keep you warm until we get home. Let's hurry to catch the next train."

"What about me?" asked Rylee.

"Don't you have anywhere to go?"

"Not really. Me folks are, um, out of town somewhere."

"Oh, come along then. But you must hurry."

A huge smile spread across Rylee's face.

On the train ride back to Leah's house, Amanda wondered who the mysterious lady was, who were those men, and why didn't Rylee have a place to go?

chapteR 14

"We should find out how Uncle Charlie is doing," said Amanda as she sat in front of the fire drying out.

"Perhaps we should call the hospital," suggested Leah. "He may be concerned about Rupert." She scratched the back of the big cat's neck as he curled up on her lap.

"Can we visit him?" asked Rylee.

"I could ask if Mom or Dad would take us to the hospital tomorrow. It isn't very far from here." Leah picked up the cat and went into the kitchen to ask her parents.

"Do you need to let Liam know about what happened today?" Amanda looked at Rylee.

"Ya, I texted him. I was hoping he'd come over to help figure out what's going on. I didn't much like the look of those two blokes, or that creepy hag either. We need to find out what Uncle Charlie's up to."

Leah came back into the living room. "Mom will drop us off at the hospital on her way to do the shopping and pick us up later, just as long as Amanda promises not to fall into any water again."

"Very funny." Amanda punched Leah on the shoulder. "That weird lady, she sure moved fast for her age. Do you think she was scared of those guys?"

"I figure that's who she was hiding from when we saw her on the roof." Rylee yawned. "I'm knackered. Can I get some kip? I don't mind sleeping on the settee."

"We all better get some sleep. Mom wants to take us to Windsor Castle tomorrow. More history for you, Amanda. I'll get you some blankets, Rylee."

The next morning after breakfast, Mrs. Anderson dropped the girls off at The Royal Surrey County Hospital.

They stopped at the front desk where Leah asked, "Could you please tell us where we can find a gentleman named Charlie, who was brought in two days ago with a hit on the head?"

"I'm afraid we will need a last name, luv."

Leah looked at Amanda and then Rylee. "Do we know his last name?"

"I don't. He was always just Uncle Charlie," replied Amanda.

"Blimey, if I can remember. Liam's name is Ramsbottom. Perhaps that's the old guy's name too."

The woman at the desk typed something into her computer. "Yes, we do have a Charles Ramsbottom in room 602. Take the elevator to the left and go up to the sixth floor. He will be in the second room to the right."

"Good call, Rylee." Leah flashed a grin.

"Is Ramsbottom really a name?" questioned Amanda.

They got on the elevator just as two men in dark suits got off.

"Aren't they the same two guys we saw at The Tower Zoo yesterday?" asked Amanda.

"They look the same to me," said Rylee.

Leah didn't say anything but looked concerned.

Uncle Charlie's head was wrapped in a bandage and his left eye was swollen shut. Smiling slightly, his hand shook as he took the grapes they brought him.

"Have you seen my cat?" he asked in a faint whisper. "I think those two men took my Rupert."

"It's all right, Uncle Charlie," said Rylee as she took his hand. "Leah here has Rupert at her place and he's living the life of Riley."

"I think you two girls saved my life back at Hampton Court." The old man gave a grateful look to Amanda and Leah.

"It was Rupert. He led us to you," said Amanda.

"He is one smart cat, he is."

"What did those men want, Uncle Charlie?"

"They said not to tell." The old man looked around nervously. "I'm very tired and need to sleep. Don't tell anyone you saw me." He closed his eyes.

"We should go." Leah put her hand on Amanda's shoulder.

Rylee gave Uncle Charlie a quick kiss on the cheek and, with a tear in her eye, followed her friends. Amanda put an arm around her. "He'll be OK. He's still in shock and a bit confused." She wondered what those men were doing in the hospital and if they threatened the poor old man.

Mrs. Anderson picked up the girls at the front of the hospital and asked about Uncle Charlie.

"He's doing as best as can be expected for an old fellow who'd been hit on the head. He seemed pleased that we were looking after Rupert."

"I've bought some things for a picnic so I thought we would go to Windsor, check out the castle and then, since the sun is shining, have a nice picnic." Mrs. Anderson turned onto the freeway.

"That'd be lovely. Thanks," said Rylee.

Amanda started to go over things in her mind as

the car sped down the motorway past vibrant green fields and stone cottages with bright yellow daffodils in the gardens. The pieces of the puzzle just didn't fit together. Could Uncle Charlie be involved in something dishonest? It seemed so unlikely.

Amanda was pleased to see Leah and Rylee talking about some weird band she had never heard of, but still couldn't understand why Rylee didn't have anywhere to go.

Rupert snored softly in the back seat, sprawled amongst the girls.

chapteR 15

Amanda was lost in her thoughts, when on a knoll in front of them, appeared a large round tower. A flag fluttered on top.

"The Queen must be in residence," announced Mrs. Anderson.

"How do you know that?" asked Amanda.

"The flag is flown whenever the Queen is in residence at Windsor Castle."

"You mean this is where she lives?"

"Not all the time. She has a number of houses. This is her favourite home. She tries to spend most weekends here. Queen Elizabeth often entertains important guests here too."

As they pulled into the parking lot, Amanda viewed the many turrets and stone wall parapets. "This place is incredible. Imagine calling it a house. Did Queen Victoria live here too?"

"Oh yes, she spent a lot of time here as well, with her large family. It has been the home of Kings and

Queens of England for over nine hundred years, and is the largest and oldest royal residence still in use. Let's visit the state apartments first and then you girls can view Queen Mary's Doll House." Mrs. Anderson led the way.

Leah leaned over and whispered in Amanda's ear, "We won't need a map or guide with Mom along."

Gleaming suits of armour lined the entrance walls. Some large and cumbersome while others small enough for a child. Knights, in full armour, sat on horses on each side of the grand staircase. Amanda felt like she had entered a movie set.

"Please take a picture of me and my knight in shining armour," she asked Leah.

"Oh my, he is handsome isn't he?" said Leah as she took the shot.

"You are getting quite a collection of photos to take home," said Leah's mom.

They entered a large room. Elaborate paintings and carved wood fruit decorated the walls. In the centre sat a long table, the wood so polished it could be used as a mirror.

Amanda counted twenty-five red velvet chairs on each side of the table. "Wow - that would be a lot of guests at a dinner party. My mom can't deal with four extra people for dinner."

"Well, I don't imagine your mom has a huge

kitchen staff either," explained Mrs. Anderson.

The next room bedazzled them with red velvet curtains trimmed in gold, red panels on gold walls and gold couches with red pillows. Amanda was not surprised when Mrs. Anderson called it The Crimson Drawing Room. All that red and gold made her eyes hurt.

Rylee looked out one of the massive windows overlooking a never-ending park. "Hey, there's Liam. I was hoping he'd come over."

"How did he know we were here?" asked Leah.

"I texted him, didn't I. We need to get down to him."

"Can we go to see the Doll House now, Mom? We're getting tired of all this old stuff."

"Sure, luv. You may have to wait in line to get in. I'd like to stay and look around some more. We can meet in the car park later." Mrs. Anderson went back to studying a large portrait.

Liam squirted clear gel out of a tube into his hand. He rubbed his hands together and ran them through his dark hair spiking it at the front. His face lit up when he saw the three girls come out of the castle.

"Who you trying to impress?" said Rylee as she gave him a kiss.

"Hey, a guy's gotta look good when he's meeting

three birds." Liam winked at Leah and Amanda. Leah's face went as red as the velvet curtains. "What's up with Uncle Charlie anyway?"

"We told mom we would be at the doll house so we better go there." Leah took them down a path with a sign pointing to Queen Mary's Doll House. On the way they filled Liam in.

"That all sounds dodgy, don't it?" Liam scratched his head. "I think the lady you mentioned was in the bookshop. She was looking at real old books and kept looking around as if she'd lost something. I didn't think much about it at the time. Lots of odd ducks come into the store."

There was a line up at the doll house but soon they were inside the building that housed it. They were allowed to walk all around the small house protected behind a rail.

"Take your time," instructed the guide. "You don't want to miss anything."

Amanda squealed with delight. Before her stood a replica of Windsor Castle, in miniature, completely furnished. The entrance with the marble staircase, the dining room with the long table set for dinner with tiny dishes, the paintings hanging on the walls and the sparkling chandeliers where all there. A library with mini books on the shelves, the nursery with toys scattered about and even a puppet theatre, caught her attention.

"Look here," Liam shouted. "There is even a garage with six fancy cars, a bicycle and a motorcycle too. They're all in perfect scale too. Blimey, I bet they even run."

"There is so much to look at," said Leah. "Look at the little paint box and book of nursery songs, the teeny mirror and hair brush set. It's so adorable."

"This would have been so much fun to play with. Do you think the princesses were allowed to play with it?" asked Amanda.

Rylee looked at the miniature garden with three inch trees and small shrubs. "Here's a baby pram and look, birds in the trees and - even a cat."

"Oh, I do hope Rupert is all right in the car," said Leah.

Mesmerized by the scene before her, Amanda felt like she had entered the land of *Lilliputians* from *Gulliver's Travels*. She wanted to disappear into the miniature building or become a princess who could spend hours playing with it.

"Amanda, Amanda," Leah tugged at her sleeve. "We should go now."

The sun shone fiercely when they emerged from viewing the doll house. Amanda rubbed her eyes. "This is bright, isn't it?" She rubbed her eyes again. "Is that her?"

"Is that who?" asked Liam and Leah at the same time.

"I swear I just saw that weird lady go into the castle."

"Well, I don't know what you saw, but I saw those two blokes who were at the hospital, sneaking behind a statue in the garden," said Rylee.

"And there's Rupert. Now, how did he get out of the car?" Leah ran into the garden after him.

chapter 16

Amanda couldn't decide whether to follow Leah or go back into the castle and find the mysterious lady. Liam and Rylee appeared nervous as they surveyed the garden.

"Let's get outta here." Liam took hold of Rylee's hand and pulled her away from the garden.

From out of nowhere, a tall, bald man wearing a dark suit and sunglasses blocked their way. "You're not going anywhere, son. Not until you tell us where the missing book from Osborne House is."

"We don't know nothing about no missing book." Liam tried pushing the man aside. "Just let us pass."

"We know you work in the old guy's bookstore. He was supposed to deliver some books to us, including the missing one. He didn't deliver them to our contact." The man glowered at Liam. "We want the book – now!"

Rupert darted out from behind a stone statue, almost knocking the tall man over. The second man, with a terrified Leah held tightly in his grip, followed. "Look what I found in the garden. Perhaps she'll tell us what we need to know."

"Leave her be. She doesn't know nothin'," said Liam.

"I don't believe she does." The tall man motioned to the other man to release Leah and looked back at Liam, "But you do, don't you?"

Liam gave a huge shove and got past the man. He dashed down the path. Both men chased after him and soon overtook him. With two guys bigger than him on each side, Liam's legs barely touched the ground as they whisked him away.

"OMG! Where are they taking Liam?" Amanda couldn't believe her eyes.

"And, where's Rupert?" asked a shaken Leah as she rubbed her wrist.

"I saw him run in there." Rylee pointed to the castle entrance.

Amanda and Leah dashed toward the castle.

Rylee looked down the path Liam had just been on, shook her head, then followed the girls into the fortress.

The three girls entered a large room; all in green.

"These are like theme rooms," said Amanda.

"There he is. Rupert is under that big, green chair," shouted Leah.

"All the chairs are green," said Amanda as she looked under the nearest one. No Rupert. "Pussy cat, pussy cat, where have you been?" Amanda started to repeat the old nursery rhyme.

"He's been to Windsor to visit the Queen." Rylee joined in.

"This isn't funny." Leah picked up Rupert and held him tightly. "Those men are - scary."

"What do you think they will do to Liam? Torture him?" asked Rylee.

"Don't be silly. This isn't exactly the middle ages. They don't use the rack anymore. Honestly."

Amanda decided the encounter with the guy in the garden had put Leah in a very bad mood.

A security guard entered the room. "I am sorry. We cannot allow pets in the castle."

"The Queen has her Corgi dogs, doesn't she?" commented Leah.

"Well, yes she does, and she loves them well enough. But, there is a special place in the castle just for them. They even have sterling silver bowls for food and water, and plush beds." The guard chuckled. "But, we cannot have pets in the state rooms."

"That's all right, we were just leaving." Leah started toward the door.

A tourist stopped to ask the security guard a

question just as the older lady from the Tower of London appeared. She looked harassed.

"I need to speak to you girls." Her eyes were hard and mean. "You are keeping something from me and I want it."

Rupert, his claws out, started to hiss. Leah couldn't hold on to him. He jumped out of her arms and lunged at the lady.

"Get that cat away from me," she screamed. She turned and headed for the front door just as the two men entered the building. In desperation, she backed up and darted down a hallway. Amanda, Rylee and Leah followed her. They turned into another room. The heel of Rylee's boot caught on the edge of the carpet. She fell down, pulling the carpet up.

"What's this?" Amanda noticed a door on the floor with a large, flat, round handle. She pulled the handle up and gave it a tug. The cellar door opened to reveal a set of dark, stone stairs. "Quick, they won't find us if we go down here."

All four plus Rupert scuttled down the stairs. Amanda pulled the door shut behind her, after making sure the carpet covered it. They heard loud, heavy footsteps thunder overhead. They held their breath until the footsteps faded away.

"This must be a secret passageway!" exclaimed

Amanda. "We should be safe here."

"We can't stay here forever. Mom will start looking for us and be worried. Why does this always happen to us?" Leah looked over at the older woman shivering in a corner. "And what about her?"

The woman looked wild-eyed. "I don't mean to hurt you. I just need to find that book those men want. The old man, Charlie, promised it to me. If I don't get it to them, I don't know what they will do to me. Or you." She shivered again. "I'm allergic to cats and they don't seem to like me for some reason. Especially that one, he hates me." She glanced at Rupert glaring at her, the tufts on the ends of his ears sticking up like antennas.

"What do you know about the missing book?" Amanda demanded.

"Not now, Amanda. We need to get out of here."

"I read a book about these secret passages once. You see, they were built so the army could escape from the castle when it was under attack. Then, they could sneak up on the enemy and attack 'em from behind. They were ever so clever those old blokes."

"You read a book about the medieval wars?" Leah looked surprised.

"'Course I did." Rylee glared at Leah. "I'm not a thick prat like you all think. I didn't go to a fancy grammar school like you, but I went to school and learned history and all that."

Leah looked away. "I'm sorry... I didn't mean to..."

"Forget it." Rylee turned to Amanda. "What now?"

"Let's follow the passageway and see where it leads." Amanda led the way.

"Maybe we can find where they took Liam," said Rylee.

"Perhaps it will take us to the car park where Mum will be waiting," sighed Leah.

"Just keep that cat away from me," said the lady as she trailed a safe distance behind.

Rupert ran ahead of everyone, like a scout ensuring the coast was clear.

chapter 17

The steps led to a dark, musty passageway. The foursome had to hold onto the wall and each other, to make their way through the dangling cobwebs, tripping over lumps of unknown substances. After what seemed a long time, they saw a faint light ahead.

"Thank heaven," said Leah as they approached another door. "I was beginning to think we were never going to get out of here."

Amanda gave the moss covered door a shove. "It won't budge. It must be stuck."

"Or locked." Rylee gave it a try, to no avail.

"Let's all try together," suggested Amanda.

With the weight of all four pushing on it, the door burst open. Everyone tumbled out into an open meadow overflowing with sunlight.

"Wow, is it ever great to see the sun again. I feel like I've been in a dungeon for years." Amanda rubbed her eyes as they adjusted to the bright sunlight. "We've come up behind the castle walls. You were right, Rylee." She picked a cobweb out of her hair.

"If those two guys are the enemy, we should be able to sneak up behind them and rescue Liam." Leah smiled at Rylee.

"You'd think." The older girl smiled back.

They walked along the back of the high, stone castle wall until they came across a thick cluster of bushes.

"Look, I think we can get through here." Amanda pointed to a small opening in the shrubs.

Everyone, except the woman, squeezed through. Sure enough, just like Rylee predicted, the two men were there, standing with their backs to them. Feet apart, arms crossed, they surveyed the park as if looking for Waldo.

Amanda put her finger to her lips and pointed to a large church. She led the others along the row of shrubs. Everything was going great until Rupert dashed out of the shrubs and around the men's legs.

"What the devil! Where did that stupid cat come from?" shouted one of the men.

They both turned and looked towards the shrubs.

"There they are! Let's get those yobs." Both men sprinted towards the young girls.

Amanda and her friends ran as fast as they could

around the corner, up the stone steps and into St. George's Chapel.

They entered a large room surrounded with huge stained glass windows that filled the chapel with a kaleidoscope of colours. Beautiful music coming from another room drew their attention. They went into the other room and noticed a group of young boys singing like angels.

"That must be the choir boys practicing," commented Leah as she scooped up Rupert before he disturbed the music.

"Do you think those guys followed us in here?" asked Rylee as she looked over her shoulder.

"I don't know, but let's hide to be safe."

Amanda opened a small door that led to a flight of stairs. The girls climbed up to an alcove with a window looking upon a courtyard. They could see the two men looking behind bushes and around statues.

"I don't think they know we're in here."

"But how are we gong to get out without them seeing us?" said Leah.

"Let's see where else these stairs lead. By the way, where is Rylee?"

Amanda and Leah started up the stairs and turned sideways to let a monk, a hood covering most of his face, pass them on the narrow stairs. The monk threw back his hood and laughed. "Got you, didn't I?" giggled Rylee.

"Where did you find that outfit?" asked Leah.

"In a room, up the stairs. I figure we can sneak out in disguise."

A few minutes later, no one noticed a monk and two choir boys emerge from the staircase, venture to the front door and down the long stone steps of the cathedral.

"There's Mum by the car." Leah started to run towards the car park.

"Whatever have you girls been up to? Why are you dressed like that? I wanted to have a picnic, but I didn't know where you had got to. And the cat is not in the car." Mrs. Anderson wrung her hands.

"It's OK, Mum, Rupert is with us. We were asked to join a little pageant in the chapel. We realized we were late, and forgot to take off the costumes." Leah pulled her choir gown off over her head and shook out her pony tail.

Mrs. Anderson took a picnic basket and a blanket out of the car. They found a flat, green patch of grass and spread out the blanket. Everyone feasted on the wonderful goodies Leah's mom brought along: sausage rolls, Cornish pasties and egg salad sandwiches. Rupert licked clean the can of tuna, brought especially for him, and then smacked his lips.

Just as they bit into the fresh strawberry tarts, the older woman staggered toward them and fell into the middle of the picnic. She picked herself up and mumbled an apology.

"Some people are ever so clumsy," said Mrs. Anderson as she shook her head.

Leah and Rylee looked after the woman in disbelief.

Amanda noticed a small, folded, piece of paper on the blanket. She unfolded it and read,

I KNOW WHERE THEY ARE KEEPING THAT BOY

She gulped and quickly put the piece of paper in her jeans pocket.

"Let's eat up so we can watch the changing of the guards." Leah's mom began to put things back in the wicker basket.

chapter 18

"We've got to find Liam." Rylee whispered in Amanda's ear as they placed the picnic things in the trunk of the car.

"You might want to read this." Amanda handed the note to Rylee.

"Come along, girls. We don't want to miss it." Mrs. Anderson waved at them to follow her. Leah rolled her eyes as she hung onto Rupert and trailed after her mother. Amanda and Rylee had no choice but to go along.

Down the centre street of the town came a marching band, wearing oversized fur hats that looked like woolly animals, perched on top of their heads. They marched past the castle entrance and through an iron gate into a green courtyard, where they stopped and continued to play music. Serious looking soldiers with the same furry hats marched behind them. Two soldiers met in the middle of the courtyard and exchanged something that looked like a huge ring of keys.

Mrs. Anderson leaned over and explained to Amanda, "These are the guards of the official residences of the Queen. The Captain of the old guard has just given the keys to the castle to the Captain of the new guard. The new sentries will now be posted."

Soldiers marched to where solitary guards, under black and gold doorways with ER printed above, stared straight ahead. New guards replaced them, while the previous guards fell into line. Amanda thought they looked very striking in their black and red uniforms, but wondered why they didn't smile.

As if reading her thoughts, Leah's mom said, "They are instructed not to smile, no matter what."

'I guess it's serious business guarding a queen,' thought Amanda.

As the retiring guard marched back through the castle gates, a young soldier looked straight at Amanda and winked. She turned beet red.

"I think he fancies you," said Leah.

Everyone laughed.

"I'm going to St. George's Chapel to listen to the choirboys," announced Mrs. Anderson.

"We've already been there and heard them," said Leah. "We'll just look around the gift shop."

"I'll meet you at the car in thirty minutes." Mrs.

Anderson walked in the direction of the chapel.

"We have thirty minutes to find Liam," said a frantic Rylee.

"How are we going to do that?" asked Leah.

Amanda pulled the note out of her jeans pocket and passed it to Leah.

"So, if we find the strange woman, we'll find Liam?" Leah looked around. "This could be a trick you know."

"We can't just leave him to the mercy of those two guys." Amanda looked in the direction of the shop. "Let's start by looking in the gift shop, like we said."

The crowded shop teemed with tourists and shelves of souvenirs like Windsor Castle salt and pepper shakers and money banks in the shape of castle guards.

Amanda gasped. Behind a shelf of miniature knights, she spotted the woman who had left the note. She dashed around the counter and grabbed the woman by her arm.

"Hey, you said you know where they are keeping Liam. Where is he?"

The woman shook off Amanda's hand and said in a low voice, "In a small warehouse behind the gift shop." She pointed towards the back of the store.

"Come with us." Amanda reached for the woman's arm again but she pulled it back.

Cling! Clang! An army of shiny knights on horseback toppled onto the floor. Many of the knights fell off their horses and lost their helmets. With spears and shields scattered everywhere, it looked like the scene of a battlefield. The store clerk rushed over.

"What are you girls doing? Can't you see the sign not to touch anything?" She bent over to pick up the fallen knights before anyone stepped on them.

The girls decided it was a good opportunity to exit the store. They ran around the back of the shop and noticed a small building.

"Let's hide from the store clerk in here," suggested Rylee looking over her shoulder.

The door opened easily. They found themselves in a dark, stuffy room filled with many boxes.

"Could this be the warehouse that woman mentioned?" asked Amanda.

"What is that noise?" asked Leah.

Rupert jumped out of her arms and ran over to a stack of boxes. He started scratching under them and meowing. Amanda heard it too, a low moaning sound.

The door of the warehouse opened.

One of the men they were trying to avoid stormed in. "Here you are. You thought you could hide from us. Instead you walked right into our trap." He slammed the door behind him. "Tell us where the book is and you won't be harmed."

"We don't know where the stupid book is, you vile lout," said Rylee. "And what have you done with Liam?"

"You'd like to see him, would you? Well he'll be pleased to have some company." The man shoved aside a stack of boxes and opened a small door. Lying on the dirt floor, with his feet and hands bound; lay a gagged Liam, moaning.

"Liam, are you OK?" Amanda ran to him. The man pushed Leah and Rylee in behind her and closed the door. The space was small; Leah and Rylee couldn't stand up in it. The man tied the girls' hands behind their back and pulled out old rags to gag them.

"You can stay in here until you decide to tell us where that book is. I'm not convinced you don't know where it is."

"My mum will come looking for us," said Leah.

"Shut up. She will never find you here." The man tied a rag over Leah's mouth. "The sooner you tell me, the sooner you can go back to your mummy." With an evil grin, he backed out of the space. "I'll be back for your answer after you've had time to think about it."

Soon Amanda's eyes became accustomed to the dark. She wriggled her fingers but the rope wouldn't budge. 'Now what are we going to do?' She tried not to think of the claustrophobic space and what might happen when the men returned.

She heard scratching, and then something soft and warm brushed past her. Her first thought was of a rat, but then she remembered Rupert might have come in with them. She could make out the shadow of a large cat as he scratched under the door. Then to her amazement, Rupert stood up on his back legs and put his front paws around the doorknob. Amanda couldn't believe it but Rupert was actually turning the knob. Soon the door burst open letting in a stream of light. She shuffled over to the open door and kicked at the boxes in front of it. When the space became big enough for her small body, she squeezed through into the main warehouse.

Amanda pushed against the front door to the warehouse with her shoulder. It opened easily and she fell out, landing at the feet of the guard who had winked at her.

chapteʀ 19

"What have we here?" asked the surprised young man as he helped Amanda to her feet and proceeded to remove the gag.

Amanda gasped for air. "My friends... my friends are in there, behind the boxes. Please help me get them out before they...they come back."

"Before who comes back?" The young man took out a Swiss army knife and cut the ropes binding Amanda's hands.

"It's a long story; can I tell you after we get my friends out?"

Just then a frazzled Leah came through the door. Amanda ran to her and removed her gag. "Can you cut her rope as well?"

"My goodness, how many more are in there?"

"Just two more, and a cat."

They quickly removed Rylee and Liam from the small space and moved the boxes back in front of it.

Leah looked at her watch. "It's time to get back to

the car."

"Thanks for all of your help – sir," stammered Amanda. She wasn't sure how to address a guard of the Queen's castle. "Don't tell anyone you saw us - please."

The guard smiled and winked at her again. "Your secret is safe with me. Stay out of trouble now."

The foursome arrived at the car at the same time as Mrs. Anderson.

Leah looked at Rylee, "We did it in thirty minutes, didn't we?"

They high-fived.

"And who is this young man," asked Leah's mom.

Liam looked pale, his hair a mess and his clothes dusty from lying on the dirt floor. He managed a faint smile.

"He's a friend of Rylee's, Mum. Can we give him a ride into town?"

"Of course. The more the merrier. Where's the cat?"

As if he heard, Rupert appeared out of nowhere, jumped into the open car and waited for everyone else to get in before settling on Leah's lap. She snuggled him close and whispered, "You are the hero of the day, my love."

After dropping Liam and Rylee off at the Guildford Tube station, the weary travelers arrived home.

Mr. Anderson met them at the door with news that he was to be in the sailboat race on the weekend, and he needed to go to the Isle of Wight immediately to get ready.

"You go ahead, luv. We will be over to watch the race on Saturday." Mrs. Anderson gave her husband a kiss on the cheek.

He picked up his duffle bag and said, "See you girls in a couple of days. Enjoy your trip into town tomorrow."

Amanda, Leah and her Mom arrived at the tube station the following cool and drizzly morning. Amanda giggled every time she saw the sign, MIND THE GAP written in large, white letters, behind a yellow line on the floor at the edge of the platform. A large arrow pointed to the space between the edge of the platform and the door of the subway car.

"What's so funny?" asked Leah.

"LOL. It just sounds weird - mind the gap."

"I think you're weird. LOL." Leah laughed and hooked her arm around Amanda's as they entered the crowded car.

They were soon in the busy streets of downtown London. Amanda was getting used to the British accents, looking the opposite way before crossing the street and seeing old brick buildings.

Entering a large intersection, Amanda stood mesmerized as tons of traffic, red double-decker buses and black taxi cabs sped around the traffic circle. Tall buildings covered in brightly coloured digital billboards, that changed quickly from one ad to the next, surrounded her.

"Welcome to Piccadilly Circus," said Leah's mom.

"A circus?"

"In this case it means a round open space at a street junction."

"I think it means it's a circus because there are always so many people here," said Leah with a grin.

"Will we go on a double-decker bus sometime?" asked Amanda.

"Sure, we can catch one right here. It will take us past some of the sights and we can get off at a lovely tea room."

Amanda loved the ride on the bus and in spite of a light rain, insisted on sitting on top. She took pictures of all the sights they passed. She thought she saw the older woman who had led them to the trap, cross the street. But, there were many women with grey hair, round glasses and beige trench coats; so she dismissed the thought.

Mrs. Anderson came up from downstairs and announced that it was time to get off the bus. The bus dropped them off in front of a white building with turquoise tables and chairs in front. The sign above the door said:

THE DISH RAN AWAY WITH THE SPOON

"OMG! This is adorable!" Amanda read the sandwich board outside, "*Come in and treat your Mum to a delicious choice of cupcakes.* I guess we will be treating you, Mrs. Anderson."

Inside, the tea shop was warm and cozy. The walls were lined with a collection of old and interesting teapots. Amanda loved the one in the shape of a thatched roof house, and another in the shape of a dragon. The glass display case featured an amazing assortment of cupcakes. Although it was difficult, Amanda decided on a vanilla cupcake with mile-high lime green, swirly icing topped with pink and red sprinkles. It looked too good to eat. She took a picture of it before biting in.

"This is so good. I may have to have another one."

The tea arrived covered in a bright pink knitted tea cozy that looked like a toque.

"This will sure keep the tea warm," Amanda said as she poured tea into a dainty teacup. She looked up and saw the woman in the trench coat staring in the window right at them. A chill went through her.

chapter 20

After polishing off three cupcakes and two cups of tea, Amanda left the tea shop with Leah and her mother. They meandered down the cobblestone street and came upon a store called

THE MARCH HARE BOOKSHOP

"Can we go in here?" asked Amanda.

"Why don't you girls look in the bookshop while I pick up something at the tailor's?" said Mrs. Anderson.

The bright, clean store had all sorts of books lined up neatly on wooden shelves. Many were behind locked glass doors. 'Nothing like Uncle Charlie's bookstore,' thought Amanda. She noticed most of the books were for children.

"May I be of assistance," asked a grandmotherly woman behind the counter.

"Are these all old books?" asked Amanda.

"Yes, this is a vintage bookstore. I collect old

children's books and sell them. Some are over one hundred years old."

"Where do you get them?"

"I find them in various places. I visit old homes, antique sales, and boot sales. Sometimes people bring them to me."

"What's a boot sale?" Amanda envisioned many boots for sale, but couldn't understand where books fit in.

Leah jumped in, "A boot sale is when people sell stuff from the boot of their car, or the trunk as you call it."

Amanda thought that was funny. "Are these books expensive?"

"Oh yes, some are over one hundred pounds," replied the storekeeper. "I have to be careful that they are authentic, as there are some clever book forgers around these days."

"Do you have any *Vicky and Alice* books?" asked Amanda.

"Not at the moment, but I am expecting some soon. Did you know those books were written for Queen Victoria's daughters? How do you know about them?"

"My great aunt had some in her book collection in Canada. She would let me read them when I visited. I also bought one on the Isle of Wight last week.

We saw the set at Osborne House too, but one was missing."

The woman turned pale. "One was missing? That's not a good sign."

Someone walked into the store. Amanda had a feeling she knew who it was. She turned to meet the eyes of the woman in the trench coat.

"Hello, Gloria. Do you have any books for me today?" asked the shopkeeper.

"Not today, I'm afraid. I've had a spot of bad luck lately. The old man who I was supposed to meet with the books, didn't show up and now I am being pursued by a couple of thugs."

"What do they want from you, Gloria?"

"They think I have the missing novel from Osborne House. I'm not sure why they want it so badly, but they are willing to pay me a large sum of money for it."

"These young ladies were just talking about the missing *Vicky and Alice* book."

Gloria glared at Amanda and Leah with steely eyes. "I think they know where it is. They are friends with the old man and his waster nephew."

"These men might be the book forgers the police have been looking for. Gloria, how did you ever get caught up with them?"

"You know I need the money badly." Gloria

tugged at the strands of grey hair that escaped her bun. "I'm in a right mess, aren't I?"

Just then, Leah's mother stuck her head in the door. "Ready to go, girls?"

"Where are we going next?" asked Amanda as they got back on to the bus.

"Next stop - the London Eye," announced Mrs. Anderson.

Amanda thought about the conversation in the bookstore. She felt sorry for the older lady called Gloria. 'No wonder she looks so miserable all the time. Were those two guys really book forgers? Did they take old books and copy them to look like they were old and then sell them for lots of money?'

She looked out the bus window and lost all thoughts of Gloria and book forgers when she saw a giant Ferris wheel at the side of the river.

"Are we going on that?"

"Oh, yes," answered Leah as they got off the bus. "That's the London Eye. It will be loads of fun. Come on, let's get in line."

When they got closer to the enormous Ferris wheel, Amanda noticed space age-like capsules moving around the wheel. She counted thirty-two of them. When it was their turn to enter a capsule, Amanda thought the wheel would stop. But it didn't, and she had to take an extra big step to get on. The spacious, glass enclosed pod held about two dozen people and everyone got a good view. Some people sat in the middle on a wooden bench.

Amanda asked a woman with a small child if she wanted to stand nearer the window. The woman said, "Thank you very much, but I have vertigo. I was told if I stay in the middle, it wouldn't affect me. I can see quite well from here."

As the wheel continued to turn slowly and smoothly, the capsule moved higher up and Amanda beheld a spectacular view of London.

"There's London Bridge," pointed Leah.

"Oh, and I see Tower Bridge," said Amanda.

"Can you see St. Paul's Cathedral over there?" mentioned Mrs. Anderson. "You can stride around to get different views of London if you like."

The little child left his mother's side and squealed, "There's Big Ben, Mummy!"

The higher they got, the farther they could see. Amanda moved from one side of the glass bubble to the other so she could see as much as possible. She felt as if she was on the top of the world. The boats on the river looked like little toy boats. Cars and buses on the bridges looked like Matchbox toys.

The morning clouds had drifted away making it a clear day. When they got to the very top, Mrs. Anderson put her arm around Amanda and pointed in the distance, "If you look over there, you will see Windsor Castle."

Amanda was amazed. She couldn't believe she could see that far. "How high up are we?"

"I believe the London Eye is 442 feet tall."

After thirty minutes they neared the ground. Amanda couldn't take it all in. She wished they could go around again. Then, on the street below, she spotted a girl with a bright pink Mohawk, tall black boots and a tight leather skirt, holding onto an old man with a bandage around his head. A young man with spiky hair and arms covered in tattoos clutched the old man's other side. Not far behind, two men in black suits and sunglasses dodged pedestrians.

chapter 21

Amanda closed her eyes tightly and then looked again. Yup, she saw right, Rylee and Liam dragged Uncle Charlie down the street with the villains in close pursuit. She grabbed Leah's hand and pulled her out of the pod while it still moved.

"We've got to help Rylee and Liam."

"Wha - What?" asked a confused Leah.

"Those men are chasing Rylee and Liam, and Uncle Charlie. We've got to do something - fast."

"Stop those men!" shouted Amanda as she sprinted down the crowded street. "Stop those two men in black suits."

People stopped and stared at her. There were many men in black suits on the street.

Amanda didn't see the trash can in front of her and smashed right into it. It toppled over spilling garbage everywhere. Leah slipped on a rotten apple.

"Yuk!" She picked herself up and brushed rubbish off her jeans. "I wish you would watch were you were going, Amanda."

Amanda kept running. She lost sight of the men. At an intersection, she barely slowed down, looked left, right and then left before putting one foot on the pavement.

"Amanda! Watch out!" shouted Leah as she grabbed her friend's arm and pulled her back onto the sidewalk. A bright red MINI Cooper zoomed by barely missing Amanda.

"What are you doing? You almost got yourself killed." Leah was shaking as she held onto Amanda.

"I- I just didn't want those two men to get away?"

"Do you mean these two men?"

The girls turned around to see who was talking. A young man with two angry men in black suits stood behind them. Handcuffed, those guys weren't going anywhere.

"We've been looking for these blokes for some time. Thanks for leading us to them."

"How did we do that?" asked Leah. "And who are you?"

Amanda recognized the young man as the guard at Windsor Castle.

"I'm Detective Inspector Sean Collins, Metropolitan Police, Crimes Investigation Division." He displayed his badge for proof.

"I thought you were a Queen's Guard?"

"I was, yesterday, while I was working under-cover."

Just then Rylee and Liam arrived with Uncle Charlie in tow.

"Thanks to your friends here, we've been able to track these two rogues and finally apprehend them. They're off to the nick now."

A police car screamed around the corner and parked on the sidewalk. A large crowd gathered to watch the two men being placed into the back of the car, glowering at Amanda and Leah.

"What is going on?" asked a disheveled Mrs. Anderson as she arrived on the scene, out of breath. "And why do you smell like rubbish?" She turned her nose up at Leah.

"Let's go for tea and I will explain," said DI Collins. He winked at Amanda again.

She felt her face go beet red and wished he wouldn't do that.

Amanda sipped on a lemonade as the young police officer explained things.

"Seems these blokes have been forging books and selling them to vintage book stores. But they needed a go-between so as not to get caught. They would get desperate folks to steal books for them or buy them cheap from an unwitting bookstore owner like unfortunate Mr. Ramsbottom here. We were tipped off that they wanted a *Vicky and Alice* book and were willing to pay a large sum of money for one of the originals from Osborne House. So, we got young Liam here to steal one."

"What!" Amanda and Leah said at the same time.

Amanda frowned at Liam, "So it was you who stole the book all along?"

"Oh yes," said the detective. "But we asked him to do it. We knew the book forgers would come looking for it and then we could nab them. What we didn't know was that Mr. Ramsbottom, Uncle Charlie, had made a deal with a woman named Gloria to sell her some of his vintage books, which she planned to sell to the book forgers. We just didn't figure things would take the turn of events they did, endangering the lives of you youngsters, and putting Mr. Ramsbottom in the hospital when they discovered he didn't have the book."

"But how did Uncle Charlie get out of the hospital?" asked Leah.

"Somebody called on my mobile this morning saying they were from the hospital, and Uncle Charlie was being discharged, and would we come and pick him up. After we did, those thick prats started to follow us. It was getting harder and harder to lose them. Man was we glad when the Met showed up," explained Liam.

Uncle Charlie looked better once he had a cup of tea. "I'm awful sorry for the bother, guv. I just needed some extra cash as the store's not doing too well these days. I didn't mean to do anything dishonest. I've never done anything dishonest in me life."

Rylee patted his arm. "You're all right now. Don't you worry."

"What about that woman, Gloria, will she be in trouble too?" asked Amanda.

"She will get a stern talking to. People do odd things when they get desperate for money. I hope this hasn't put you off England, Amanda."

"Oh no, sir. I think it's awesome I got to meet a real British Bobby, but why aren't you wearing a uniform?"

"Those of us in the CID are plain clothes detectives, so we blend in. We only wear our uniforms for special occasions. I best be off now. We'll be in touch Liam and Rylee. Thanks for your help. Mrs. Anderson, Leah, it was nice to meet you. Enjoy the rest of your visit Amanda and - stay out of trouble."

"As if," muttered Leah.

"What did you say?" asked Amanda.

"I said, I still smell as if I fell into a rubbish tip. I

need to get home and have a bath."

$$\Rightarrow \Leftarrow$$

On the weekend, Amanda, Leah and Mrs. Anderson watched the Isle of Wight sailboat races from the shore. Amanda cheered the loudest as the *Shelagh* came in first place. After the race the girls walked over to the bookstore.

The store looked much brighter and cleaner.

"Hi ya!" greeted Liam from on top of a ladder.

"Wowza," said Leah. "I hardly recognized the place."

"Well, I reckon if I'm going to be managing the store now, I want it to be more attractive to customers." Liam started down the ladder.

A well dressed, young girl with short black hair emerged from behind a stack of books, a feather duster in her hand.

"Who is this?" asked Amanda.

"I'm the part-time Assistant Manager," answered Rylee with a huge grin. "I'm about to organize these books according to the alphabet, so folks can find what they're looking for."

She gave Leah and Amanda each a big hug. "You'll never guess. I'm living at Liam's mum's place now and will be going back to school part-time. You two mates were ever so nice to me and made me feel

I was maybe worth something. I want to be smart like you, Leah and kind like you, Amanda."

"Where is your family, Rylee?" Amanda just had to ask.

Rylee looked away and mumbled. "They're not around. Don't know when they'll be back."

Leah quickly changed the subject. "How's Uncle Charlie?"

"Oh he's fine. He loves the old folks' home he's living in now. He misses Rupert though," said Liam.

"Tell him Rupert is fine and getting loads of attention at our house," said Leah. "I'll bring him for a visit one day soon. Maybe you could come along, Rylee."

Rylee beamed. "I would love that."

After tearful goodbyes at the bookstore, Amanda and Leah walked arm-in-arm down the cobblestone street.

"Well, things certainly worked out OK, didn't they," said Amanda. "You got a cat, Liam got a job, Rylee got a home and I had a great time in England. I can't wait to show everyone at home the fab pictures I took."

"The only bad thing is you're going home soon, and I don't know when we'll see each other again?" Leah looked teary eyed.

"Well, we can keep in touch on Facebook and

text each other too." Amanda thought for a minute. "Why don't you come and visit me? We could have tons of fun exploring Alberta. There's a dinosaur park and the Calgary Stampede and so much cool stuff to do. There's never any crime or people in trouble so you wouldn't have to worry about being chased or anything like that."

"That sounds like a plan BFF. But knowing you, I'm sure you'll scare up a mystery - just for me?"

THE END

acknowledgements

I would like to acknowledge the many people who have helped me bring Amanda in England – the Missing Novel to life. My heartfelt thanks go out to my critique partners near and far, Yvonne, Marion, Cyndy and Sheila. I don't know what I would have done without your eye for detail and your inquiring minds. I also want to thank Brenda for the idea of a Maine Coon cat, Avril for sharing pictures of Hampton Court, Alison for the idea of the teashop, Terry and Linda for the ride on their sailboat and Lizzie for telling me what it was like to ride the London Eye. I mustn't forget my many English friends for consultation on British words and phrases and of course my wonderful English husband, Paul, who patiently clarified a number of things.

A huge thank you to all the young people who have become fans of Amanda and her adventures. You inspire and motivate me. A multitude of thanks go out especially to Michelle Halket, Publisher at Central Avenue Publishing, for all the support and encouragement over the past few years. You are the best!

The Vicky and Alice Books do not exist; they come entirely out of my imagination. The ravens at the Tower of London do exist, as does Queen Mary's Doll House at Windsor Castle and the Royal Menagerie at the Tower of London. The Dish Ran Away with the Spoon is a teashop in Manchester; I simply moved it to London for the purpose of my story.

also by darlene foster

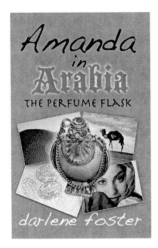

Amanda Ross is an average twelve year old Canadian girl. So what is she doing thousands of kilometres from home in the United Arab Emirates? It's her own fault really, she wished for adventure and travel when she blew out those candles on her last birthday cake. Little did she know that a whole different world awaited her on the other side of the globe, one full of intrigue, mystery and folklore. A world with a beautiful princess, a dangerous desert and wonderful friends.

Join Amanda on her first adventure as she discovers the secrets behind The Perfume Flask.

Amanda Jane Ross is certainly becoming a world traveller; she's now in sunny Spain on vacation with her friend Leah. While there, she encounters a mysterious young girl who looks eerily like the girl in a famous painting she saw in a Madrid museum. Even weirder, the girl keeps showing up wherever Amanda finds herself - Madrid, the remote mountains of rural Spain, the beaches on the Mediterranean Sea, a lively fiesta and the busy streets of Barcelona. Amanda wants to help this sweet, young girl and her beloved pony escape the clutches of a mean horse-dealer. Come with Amanda on her next adventure as she attempts to unravel the mystery behind the Girl in the Painting while she treks across Spain - always one step ahead of danger!

about the author

Darlene Foster is an employment counsellor, an ESL tutor for children, a wife, mother and grandmother. She loves travel, shoes, cooking, reading, sewing, chocolate, music, the beach and making new friends. Her 13 year old grandson called her "super-mega-as-woman-supreme". She was brought up on a ranch near Medicine Hat, Alberta, where she dreamt of travelling the world and meeting interesting people. She lives on the west coast of BC with her husband Paul and their black cat, Monkey.

Her website is darlenefoster.ca.

CPSIA information can be obtained at www.ICGtesting.com
Printed in the USA
BVOW011714011212

307027BV00007B/275/P